CARTOON CRAZY

CARTOON NETWORK™

by E. S. Mooney
Based on
"THE POWERPUFF GIRLS,"
as created by Craig McCracken

SCHOLASTIC INC.

New York   Toronto   London   Auckland   Sydney
Mexico City   New Delhi   Hong Kong

ISBN 0-439-16021-9

Design by Peter Koblish
Cover: Mary Hall

12 11 10 9 8 7 6 5 4 3 2 1   0 1 2 3 4 5/0

Printed in the U.S.A.
First Scholastic printing, October 2000

SUGAR . . .

SPICE . . .

AND EVERYTHING NICE . . .

These were the ingredients chosen to

create the perfect little girl.

But Professor Utonium accidentally

added an extra ingredient to

the concoction —

CHEMICAL X!

And thus, The Powerpuff Girls were born!

Using their ultra superpowers,

BLOSSOM,

BUBBLES,

and BUTTERCUP

have dedicated their lives to fighting crime

and the forces of evil!

chapter 1

The city of Townsville . . .

It was another peaceful evening. The Powerpuff Girls were tired out after a long day of battling monsters. Now it was time to relax. . . .

Blossom, Bubbles, and Buttercup were sitting together on the couch in front of the TV. They were watching their favorite show, *The TV Puppet Pals.*

Mitch and Clem, the two puppets on the show, were playing hide-and-seek. It was Mitch's turn to hide, and Clem was having a tough time finding him.

Bubbles's forehead was wrinkled with concern. "I hope Clem finds Mitch soon!" Her blond pigtails trembled.

Blossom put her arm around her sister. "Don't worry," she said. "I'm sure he will."

Buttercup rolled her green eyes. "Really, Bubbles. The show is almost over. You know the *Puppet Pals* always has a happy ending."

Bubbles brightened. "Oh, yeah," she giggled. "I forgot."

Sure enough, a moment later, Clem found Mitch behind a tree. The two puppets hugged, and the show ended.

Bubbles sighed happily. "That was great."

"And now, stay tuned for a brand-new cartoon show, boys and girls," the TV announcer said. "Coming up next, it's *The Adventures of Amazonia!*"

A dark-haired woman with a giant *A* on her superhero uniform swung by on a vine. "Evildoers beware — Amazonia's here!" she cried.

Hey, look at that, Girls! A superhero, just like you!

"Wow!" Buttercup said.

"A new show!" Bubbles cried.

"It looks good," Blossom added.

Professor Utonium came into the room. "All right, Girls. Your show is over. Time to turn off the TV."

"But, Professor!" Buttercup objected.

"There's a brand-new cartoon coming on," Blossom explained.

"Can we watch it?" Bubbles asked. "Pretty please?"

"Oh, all right, Girls," the Professor said with a smile. "But after that, it's straight to bed, understand?"

The Girls didn't answer him. Their eyes were glued to the TV set as they watched Amazonia battle bad guys and monsters. In her silver boots and silver gloves, Amazonia looked really cool. She was really tough, too.

"Evildoers beware—Amazonia's here!" Amazonia cried. She sent streaming vines out of the wrists of her silver gloves. The vines wrapped around two bad guys, binding them together.

"Yay!" Buttercup yelled. She bounced up and down on the couch.

A third bad guy was sneaking up on Amazonia from behind.

"Watch out, Amazonia!" Buttercup cried. "He's got a ray gun!"

"Buttercup, she can't hear you," Blossom pointed out.

But Buttercup didn't pay any attention to her sister. She continued watching as Amazonia pressed one of the buttons on her silver power-belt. The button activated a special antilaser shield. The bad guy's lasers bounced off her and back onto him.

"Yay!" Buttercup cheered again.

Finally, Amazonia picked up the three bad guys. She swung them around and hurled them through the air. They landed right in a jail cell. Amazonia slammed the door to the cell shut and turned to face the audience with a smile. Then the *Amazonia* theme song began playing as the final credits rolled.

"Hey, that was pretty good," Blossom commented.

"Yeah, Amazonia is cool," Bubbles agreed.

Buttercup was still staring at the TV set, her green eyes fixed on the screen.

"Buttercup?" Blossom nudged her sister. "Are you okay?"

"You liked the show, didn't you?" Bubbles asked.

Buttercup turned to face her sisters. She wore an expression of complete astonishment.

"That was the best!" she said. "Amazonia is amazing!"

A few minutes later, the Girls were tucked into their big bed. The Professor came in to say good night.

"Sweet dreams, Girls," he said, turning out the light.

"Good night, Professor!" the Girls called out.

The Girls lay in the dark.

After a moment, Buttercup spoke up. "Did you see the way she threw those bad guys around? She must be the strongest woman on the planet." She sighed. "Amazonia is the best."

The Girls lay in bed in silence.

Then Buttercup spoke up again. "And what about that cool power-belt? The button that activated the antilaser shield was great. I wonder what those other buttons on her belt do. Amazonia's amazing."

Bubbles cuddled with her stuffed octopus. "Yeah, but Octi and I still like the Puppet Pals better," she said.

Buttercup sat up in bed and turned on the light. "Are you crazy, Bubbles?" she yelled. "Amazonia is the best ever! Didn't you see the way she —"

Blossom cut her off. "Buttercup, enough! We have to get some sleep. Now turn off the light."

That's right, Buttercup. Time for bed. Remember, superheroes need their sleep!

chapter 2

The next morning . . .

The sun rose, and the Girls' eyes popped open bright and early.

"Time to say hello to a brand-new day!" Bubbles said happily.

"Time for a nourishing breakfast to give us strength!" Blossom announced.

"Time to check the TV listings and see when Amazonia's on again!" Buttercup cried, racing down the stairs ahead of her sisters.

Blossom and Bubbles looked at each other and shrugged. They flew downstairs to the kitchen.

The Professor was standing at the counter. "Good morning, Girls!" he sang out in greeting. "Where's Buttercup?"

Just then, Buttercup flew in. She was waving the TV listings in the air. "It's on again!" she yelled happily. "Amazonia's going to be on every night at seven!"

"Well, you certainly seem cheerful today, Buttercup," the Professor said, smiling. "Now, what would everyone like for breakfast?"

"I want pancakes!" Bubbles burst out. "With syrup and powdered sugar and whipped cream and a cherry!"

"Okay, sweet pancakes for my sweet

Bubbles," the Professor replied. "Blossom?"

"I'd like eggs, please," Blossom told him. "With whole wheat toast and fruit."

"A nice, healthy start to the day," the Professor commented. "Buttercup? What would you like?"

Buttercup thought for a moment. "Rattlesnakes."

"Rattlesnakes?" the Professor repeated in surprise.

"That's what Amazonia eats," Buttercup explained excitedly. "She wrestles live rattlesnakes with her bare hands and then she eats them. Their venom gives her superhuman strength."

"Amazonia is Buttercup's new favorite cartoon character," Blossom explained.

"Oh, I see," the Professor replied with a chuckle. "Well, I'm afraid we're fresh out of rattlesnakes now. But would some sausage links do instead?"

"Well, all right," Buttercup agreed.

As the Girls were finishing their breakfast, they heard a loud beeping sound.

"The hotline!" Blossom cried, jumping up from the table. The hotline was the special telephone that the Mayor of Townsville used to keep in touch with The Powerpuff Girls. Blossom picked up the receiver. "Hello?"

"Blossom, hurry!" the Mayor's voice cried. "A monster is attacking Townsville Airport! We need you Girls right away!"

"We're on our way, Mayor!" Blossom promised. She hung up and turned to her sisters. "The Mayor needs us at the airport on the double!"

With a quick wave to the Professor, the Girls flew off. As they neared the airport, they could see an enormous, gooey, orange monster stomping around on the runways. He held an airplane in each of his clawed hands.

"Come on, Girls. Let's get him!" Blossom cried.

"We're right behind you!" Bubbles replied.

"Yeah!" Buttercup took a deep breath. "Evildoers beware — Amazonia's here!" she cried.

Blossom and Bubbles stopped in their

tracks. Their mouths dropped open in surprise. "Wha — ?" they said.

But there was no time to lose. The monster was roaring and headed straight for the Girls.

The Girls flew at him. Buttercup was in the lead now, her face set in an angry scowl.

Go get him, Buttercup!

But suddenly, the monster shot bright orange lasers out of his eyes — straight at Buttercup!

Blossom and Bubbles watched as the rays headed straight for their sister.

Oh, no, Buttercup! Quick, use your superpowered eye beams to knock the lasers off course! Use your superspeed to dodge the beams! Do something! Anything!

Buttercup pressed her arms together as if she was trying to shoot vines out like Amazonia.

Buttercup, what are you doing? This is no time to play make-believe!

"Ha-ha!" Buttercup cried. "Your laser can't hurt me! I've got a silver power-belt with an antilaser shield!"

What? No, you don't, Buttercup!

"All I have to do is press this button and —" Suddenly, the laser beams hit Buttercup, throwing her backward. She crashed into the arrivals terminal and fell to the ground in a crumpled green heap.

"Buttercup, are you all right?" Bubbles cried in alarm.

Blossom swooped by and grabbed her sister. Buttercup shook her head in surprise.

"Buttercup, this is no time for games," Blossom scolded her. "Come on, let's get him!"

The monster threw down the airplanes and began swiping at the Girls.

Bubbles quickly caught one of the planes and gently set it down on the ground. Then she zoomed toward the monster's legs. She socked the monster in one of his orange knees, making him stagger. Then she grabbed one of his legs. She began wrapping it around the other leg. Soon the monster's legs were so tangled he could barely stand.

Meanwhile, Blossom caught the second airplane and placed it carefully down on the runway. Then she zipped straight into the monster's stomach, delivering a superpowered punch that knocked him to the ground.

The Goo Monster sat on the runway, stunned.

"Don't worry!" Buttercup cried, flying in toward him. "I've got him wrapped up!" But to her sisters' surprise, Buttercup flexed her muscles, pointing her arms at the monster.

Buttercup, what are you doing now?

"Watch out, goo boy. I'm going to tie you up with my wrist-vines," Buttercup threatened. She continued pointing her arms toward the monster. "Evildoers beware — Amazonia's here!"

The monster began staggering to his feet. Buttercup was still standing there, aiming her arms at him.

"Buttercup!" Blossom yelled. She sighed angrily. "Oh, forget it! Come on, Bubbles, let's get him with a victory volley."

Blossom and Bubbles flew toward the monster. Together, they began punching him in the stomach. Soon the monster was curled up in a little ball. Bubbles and Blossom tossed the balled-up monster back and forth a few times. Finally, they let him drop to the ground with a gooey *splat.*

"Ha! Told you you didn't stand a chance!" Buttercup cried triumphantly, flying over to the defeated monster. "You're history now!"

"Yeah, no thanks to you!" Blossom said, glaring at Buttercup.

Uh-oh. Looks like there's trouble between the Girls. Now, come on, Girls. You wouldn't let a little thing like a cartoon come between you, would you?

chapter 3

A few nights later, at The Powerpuff Girls' house . . .

Buttercup sat on the couch, her eyes glued to the TV.

"Go, Amazonia!" she cried. "Get them! Use your vines! Your vines!"

Bubbles flew into the room. "Excuse me, Buttercup?" she said. "I can't find Octi. Have you seen him anywhere?"

Buttercup didn't respond.

"Buttercup?" Bubbles tried again.

"Go, Amazonia, go!" Buttercup yelled again. "Hurry! Press the Invisilator button on your power-belt so they won't see you! Yes!"

Bubbles sighed. "Never mind," she said. She flew out of the room.

A few minutes later, Blossom came in. "Hey, Buttercup, guess what?" she said. "The Professor said we can make popcorn balls! Want to help?"

Buttercup continued staring at the TV.

"Buttercup?" Blossom said again. She flew over to her sister and studied her face. "Buttercup? Are you okay?"

Buttercup looked strange. Her face was pale, and her green eyes looked glazed.

"Buttercup?" Blossom said again.

Bubbles flew back into the room. "I

don't think she can hear you," she commented.

Blossom shook her head. "I know. It's like she's in some kind of TV trance."

The show ended, and the *Amazonia* theme music played. Buttercup applauded wildly.

"Well, thank goodness that's over," Blossom muttered. She glanced at the screen as the final credits began to roll. "Oh, no! Look at that!" Blossom yelled suddenly, pointing at the credits.

"What?" Bubbles asked.

"Right there!" Blossom said, pointing again. "Look at what that says!" She shook her head. "I knew there was something weird about this show!"

Bubbles squinted. "I don't get it. It says, 'Animation by Akudou Studios.'"

"No, not that!" Blossom cried. "Underneath that! Look. 'A Monkey MasterMind Production.'"

Bubbles gasped. "Oh, my gosh! Monkey MasterMind? I don't know any monkey master-minds."

"In fact, the only monkey mastermind is Mojo Jojo . . . oh, no!" Blossom declared. Mojo Jojo was the Girls' archenemy. He was an evil super-genius monkey.

"But why would Mojo want to produce a TV show?" Bubbles asked.

"I don't know, but whatever the reason is, it can't be good," Blossom replied. She turned to Buttercup. "Buttercup, you've got to stop watching this show! Do you hear me? Buttercup!"

But Buttercup was still staring at the screen, clapping. Her eyes were glassy.

"And now," the TV announcer said, "stay tuned for scenes from tomorrow's exciting *Adventures of Amazonia.*"

"Yay!" Buttercup cheered, bouncing up and down on the couch.

Suddenly, there was a loud beeping sound. "The hotline!" Blossom cried, flying over to answer the special phone.

"Girls, hurry!" the Mayor screamed. "A thief is stealing the artwork from the Townsville Museum!"

"Oh, no!" Blossom gasped. "We'll be right there," Blossom

promised the Mayor. "Bubbles, Butter-cup, come on! The Mayor needs us right away!"

"Ready to go!" Bubbles replied.

"Come on, Buttercup!" Blossom called.

But Buttercup didn't budge. She was still staring at the TV.

"Buttercup!" Blossom cried. She shook her sister by the arm. "Townsville needs us! Come on!"

Buttercup didn't even blink. Her hard, empty green eyes were glued to the screen. "Go! Go, Amazonia, go!" she yelled, watching the scenes.

Blossom sighed. "Come on, Bubbles, there's no time to waste. We'll have to do it without her."

What? The Powerpuff Girls, split up? Oh, no! Say it isn't so!

Chapter 4

Blossom and Bubbles flew at top speed toward the Townsville Museum. A huge truck was parked in front. It was loaded with paintings and sculptures.

The Mayor stood by the truck, wringing his hands. He was dressed in a black top hat and a black jacket with tails, as usual.

"Oh, Girls, thank goodness you're here!" the Mayor cried. "The thief is taking all the city's priceless artwork!" He looked around. "But wait a minute. Where's Buttercup?"

"Oh, uh — she couldn't make it," Blossom replied.

"It's kind of a long story," Bubbles added.

"Yeah . . . about a half-hour long, every night at seven," Blossom muttered.

Just then the thief came out of the museum. He wore a red-and-white-striped shirt and a sinister black mask. In one hand he held a painting of a bowl of fruit. In his other hand was a ray-blaster gun.

Blossom put her hands on her hips. "Stop, thief! You put down that priceless painting this instant!"

The thief let out a laugh. "Who's gonna make me?"

"You'll see who! Come on, Bubbles!" Blossom cried. "Let's get him!"

Together, Blossom and Bubbles flew into action. They zoomed toward the thief at full speed. The thief aimed his ray-blaster. A jagged yellow ray shot out toward the Girls.

"Watch out!" Blossom cried. "Duck, Bubbles!"

Bubbles ducked out of the way just in time. Meanwhile, Blossom zoomed around behind him. But the thief was fast. He swung around and zapped Blossom with his ray-blaster.

Blossom flew backward and landed on the ground. Bubbles flew over and landed beside her sister.

The thief took aim again.

"Okay, time for the triple — oops, I

mean double eye-beam move," Blossom directed.

Bubbles nodded. She and Blossom stared hard at the thief, directing their laser eye beams at him. The thief fired his blaster. The Girls' pink and blue eye beams collided with the jagged yellow ray from the blaster. The two forces pushed against each other and canceled each other out.

Uh-oh, Girls. Looks like your eye beams and this guy's blaster beam are exactly equal in strength! What are you going to do now?

"Must . . . send . . . out . . . stronger . . . beams. . . ." Blossom grunted, staring as hard as she could.

"I can't . . ." Bubbles panted. "I can't do any more!" She collapsed, exhausted. "It's no use! We need Buttercup!"

The thief began running away.

"Oh, no you don't!" Blossom yelled. She flew after the thief as fast as she could.

But suddenly, he stepped aside and held out the painting, right in Blossom's path. She crashed through the canvas.

The thief dropped the painting with a shrug. He hopped into his truck and drove off, leaving a cloud of exhaust behind.

The Mayor looked at Bubbles, who was still sitting on the ground, panting. Then he looked at Blossom, who was wearing the frame of the smashed painting around her neck like a necklace.

"Well, thanks for trying, Girls," he said. "But I

think you should bring Buttercup next time."

Oh, no! The Powerpuff Girls have failed? It can't be!

Meanwhile, Mojo Jojo, evil supergenius monkey and archenemy of The Powerpuff Girls, was watching it all from his brand-new, state-of-the-art TV tower atop Townsville Volcano Mountain.

Mojo sat at a large oval desk. On the desk was a plaque that said MONKEY MASTERMIND PRODUCTIONS. On the wall in front of him were twenty TV screens. Nineteen of the screens were showing what was going on in different areas of Townsville. The twentieth screen was showing *The Adventures of Amazonia.*

Mojo looked up at the TV screen that showed Blossom and Bubbles trying to battle the art thief.

"Ha-ha-ha, Powerpuff Girls!" Mojo cackled, his monkey face breaking into an evil grin. "Thanks to my evil genius TV show idea, there are now only two of you on the crime-fighting scene! And two Powerpuff Girls just aren't enough! Not enough to stop me and my evil plans! Ha-ha-ha-ha!"

Mojo watched as the thief drove away with the precious artwork.

"You see? Now the thieves and the criminals and the monsters will have their way in Townsville! And you will be powerless to stop them!" Mojo cackled again. "Then evil will defeat good, and I, Mojo Jojo, will be on top! And when I, Mojo Jojo, am on top, you, the Powerpuff Girls, will be ground beneath my boots! Ha-ha-ha-ha!"

Oh, no! So Mojo is behind this after all! Townsville's in big trouble!

chapter 5

The next day . . .

Blossom and Bubbles stood in front of
Buttercup in their room.

Blossom had her arms crossed. "Buttercup, we have to talk," she said.

Buttercup was dressed in an official licensed Amazonia superhero costume. She
was lying on her stomach playing with several
action figures from the official licensed
Amazonia superhero action figure collection.

"Evildoers beware — Amazonia's here!" Buttercup yelled. She picked up her Amazonia figure and made it attack one of the other figures.

Bubbles cringed. "Oooh, that's not a very nice way to play. Why don't you have them go to the zoo or on a picnic instead?"

Buttercup ignored her and continued her attack, making the figures wrestle on the carpet.

"Buttercup, stop playing and listen to me! There's something terrible happening!" Blossom cried.

Buttercup looked up. "I know," she said. "This Amazonia action figure is supposed to come with real shooting wrist-vines. But they're only dumb green strings. They don't even cling onto things! What a rip-off!"

Blossom stomped her foot with frustration. "Buttercup, listen to me. Mojo Jojo has some sort of evil plan and the *Amazonia* show is part of it. You've been taken under its spell and now criminals and monsters are going to take over Townsville! And without you we can't stop it!" she blurted out.

Buttercup looked up at her sister. "Don't be silly," she said. "There's no evil plot. And I'm not under any spell. *Amazonia*'s just a really great show."

"Well, then how do you explain this?" Blossom waved a piece of paper in front of Buttercup's face.

NOTICE

TO ALL CRIMINALS AND MONSTERS
INTERESTED IN DESTROYING TOWNSVILLE.

SEVEN O'CLOCK EACH NIGHT IS A VERY GOOD
TIME TO ATTACK.

SINCERELY,
A FRIEND

"They're posted all over Townsville," Bubbles said.

"You've got to snap out of it, Buttercup," Blossom added. "You've got to stop watching *Amazonia*. Don't you see what's happening?"

Suddenly, Buttercup jumped up from her spot on the floor, dropping her action figures. "Oh, my gosh, I can't believe it!"

she cried. "I was so busy playing with my action figures that I didn't even realize!"

"Finally, she's coming to her senses!" Blossom said with relief.

"It's almost seven!" Buttercup continued. She hurried over to the TV and switched it on. "I almost missed *Amazonia*! That was a close one!"

Blossom and Bubbles looked at each other and sighed.

"Hey, kids, stay tuned for *The Adventures*

of Amazonia!" the TV announcer said. "And don't forget to tune in for the all-day, all-night *Amazonia* marathon tomorrow! That's right! We'll be showing nothing but *Amazonia* cartoons from morning till night!"

"Yay!" Buttercup cheered from the couch.

"Oh, no!" Blossom and Bubbles groaned.

Blossom turned to Bubbles. "We have to do something! The monsters and criminals are going to have a field day tomorrow! Townsville's going to need all three of us to stop them!"

Bubbles's mouth trembled. "But what can we do?"

Blossom's face looked determined. "Just leave it to me. I think I have a plan. . . ."

Good going, Blossom! Townsville's depending on you!

chapter 6

Late that night . . . Oh, no! Blossom! What are you still doing up at this hour?

Blossom sat on the living room floor, behind the TV. Stacks of the Professor's technical books surrounded her. A set of tools were spread out beside her on the floor.

Blossom carefully removed the back of the TV set and went to work. She moved in a blur of hammering, sawing, cutting, drilling, screwing, and splicing. She

worked all through the night. She finally
finished just before dawn. Then she
dragged herself upstairs and fell into bed
beside her sisters.

The next morning!
Bubbles and Buttercup woke up bright
and early. Blossom was still in a deep sleep.
"Blossom?" Bubbles sounded con-
cerned. "Blossom, it's morning!" She

turned to Buttercup. "I hope she's okay. Blossom never sleeps late. She's always —"

"No time to talk," Buttercup cut her off. "I gotta get downstairs right away. The *Amazonia* marathon's about to begin." She zoomed out of the room.

"Blossom?" Bubbles patted her sister's shoulder.

Blossom opened her eyes halfway. "Hi, Bubbles. Where's Buttercup?"

Bubbles frowned. "She went downstairs to watch *Amazonia*. I guess whatever your plan was it didn't —"

"Aaaah!" Buttercup let out a scream from downstairs.

Blossom smiled. "It worked!"

"What worked?" Bubbles asked.

"My plan," Blossom explained. "I used the Professor's books and equipment to rewire the TV. I added a special feature that blocks out *Amazonia*." She smiled. "I call it the A-chip."

"Wow!" Bubbles's blue eyes glowed with admiration.

Buttercup stomped upstairs. Her eyes were wild, and her face looked panicky. "It's not on!" she cried. "It's not on! I can't find the *Amazonia* marathon anywhere on TV!"

Blossom winked at Bubbles. "Well, maybe they canceled it."

"Canceled?!" Buttercup sounded desperate.

Just then, the hotline started ringing.

"Right on schedule," Blossom commented. She zoomed off to answer it. "Hello? What's that, Mayor? There are monsters and criminals destroying Townsville? Don't worry. The Powerpuff Girls will be there in no time — all three of us!" She turned to her sisters. "Come on, Girls! Townsville needs us!"

Buttercup hesitated.

"Come on, Buttercup," Bubbles urged. "Fighting crime will take your mind off the TV."

"Well, okay," Buttercup replied. "I'm right behind you!"

As the Girls flew toward the center of town, they could hear crashes, screams, and explosions in the distance.

Blossom paused on a street corner to give her sisters a pep talk. "Girls, it sounds like every monster and criminal in Townsville is on the loose. It's going to take everything the three of us have to fight this. We'll have to —" She paused. "Buttercup? Where are you going? Oh, no!"

Across the street, at the Townsville Electronics store, the display window was filled with TVs. And all of them were tuned in to *Amazonia*! Buttercup was floating across the street as if pulled by a magnetic force.

"Buttercup, stop!" Blossom yelled.

"Come back!" Bubbles pleaded. "We have to fight crime, remember?"

But it was too late. Buttercup stood in front of the store, her face pressed to the glass. Her eyes were glued to the dozens of screens in front of her.

Blossom shook her head. "We're going to have to do it alone, Bubbles. Come on!"

Oh, no! Dozens of monsters and criminals to fight, and only two Powerpuff Girls? This doesn't look good!

Chapter 7

Blossom and Bubbles zoomed past the Townsville Bank. They saw a gang of criminals running out with bags of money. The Girls swooped down on the criminals, hitting them with rapid-fire punches.

The criminals began firing at the Girls. But Blossom and Bubbles managed to dodge the bullets with their superspeed. They paralyzed the criminals with their eye beams.

The criminals screamed, terrified. They dropped the bags of money and ran.

"Come on!" Blossom instructed, out of breath from the fight. "Let's get this green stuff back where it belongs!"

She and Bubbles grabbed the bags of money and returned them to the bank.

"Thank you, Power-puff Girls!" the people in the bank called out.

"Hey, where's Butter-cup?" they added.

But there was no time to explain. Blossom and Bubbles could hear explosions and screams in the distance. They sped off.

"Look!" Bubbles cried, pointing.

A huge green monster with giant yellow eyes was standing in the Townsville River.

He grabbed hold of the Townsville Bridge and snapped it in two. People and cars began sliding off the bridge into the river.

Blossom and Bubbles sprang into action. They dove into the river, gathering cars and people in their arms.

"Hey," the people asked as they were being saved, "where's Buttercup?"

But Blossom and Bubbles were too out of breath to answer. And the green monster was after them. He grabbed both Girls and threw them into the river with a splash.

The Girls bobbed to the surface, coughing and sputtering.

"Come on, Bubbles," Blossom called, panting and coughing. "Let's get him with the baseball blast!" She flew over and picked up one piece of the broken bridge. Bubbles grabbed another piece.

Blossom swung her piece of the bridge and hit the monster square on the head. "Strike one!" she yelled, letting her bat fly.

Bubbles did the same with her piece of the bridge. "Strike two!" she squealed.

The monster was reeling. But he managed to swipe at the Girls again, knocking them back into the water.

Bubbles surfaced beside Blossom.

"What happened?" Bubbles asked.

"I think our timing was off," Blossom answered. "Buttercup usually delivers strike three. Come on, let's work on him some more."

The Girls flew straight toward the monster, punching with all their might. Finally, they managed to knock him back into the water. He lay there like a big green island. Blossom and Bubbles had won the battle, but they were superexhausted.

"How are we ever going to do this?" Bubbles wailed. "There are monsters like this all over Townsville! We'll never beat them all alone!"

"Hey, look!" Blossom cried out. She pointed to a big new tower rising from the top of Townsville Volcano Mountain. The tower had the letters MMMP on it. "Activate your super radar vision," Blossom instructed.

With their radar vision, the Girls were able to see the wiggly waves of a TV signal. It was flowing from an antenna on the top of the tower. And it was headed straight toward Townsville.

"MMMP must stand for Monkey

MasterMind Productions," Blossom explained. "Follow that signal!"

The two Girls took off toward the tower. On the way, they passed a gang of criminals robbing the Townsville Department Store, a purple monster with fangs climbing the Townsville Trade Center, and a brown slime monster oozing all over the Townsville Sports Arena.

"Sorry, we can't help you now. But we'll be right back!" Blossom promised as she and Bubbles zoomed past the troubled citizens of Townsville.

"Hurry, Girls!" the people cried out after them. "Oh, and hey, where's Buttercup?" they added.

Finally, Blossom and Bubbles reached

the tower. They crashed through the wall and found themselves standing face-to-face with Mojo Jojo and his twenty TV screens. Nineteen of the screens were showing different areas of Townsville being destroyed. The twentieth was showing the *Amazonia* marathon.

"Mojo Jojo, I knew you were behind this!" Blossom said, pointing at the screens. "And now you're going to pay for it!"

"Yeah," Bubbles added. "'Cause what you did wasn't very nice!"

Mojo crackled evilly. "Do you really think you can defeat me, Powerless Girls? You are not even The Powerpuff Girls anymore. Because The Powerpuff Girls are a trio, and you are only a duo. Ha-ha-ha-ha!"

"Oh, yeah? Well, take that!" Bubbles cried. She shot out a baby-blue eye beam.

"Yeah, and that!" Blossom added a bright pink eye beam.

But Mojo pressed a button on the control panel of his desk. A clear, shieldlike capsule rose around him. The Girls' eye beams bounced off the shield — and onto the control panel! It exploded in a cloud of smoke. The TV screens went blank.

Mojo's face dropped. He let out a blood-curdling scream. "Aaaaah! You have destroyed my TV power center! You have destroyed my TV power center!" Then he paused. "Okay, so you have destroyed my TV power center. But that will not stop me from creating a new TV power center, with even better shows. Shows that all three of you will like so much that you will never fight again!"

Mojo pulled a lever inside his shield-capsule. The capsule rose in the air and several spikes popped out of it.

"Let's get him, Bubbles," Blossom said with determination.

The Girls flew into action. They battered against the surface of the capsule with all their might. But it was no use. They were just too tired. And there were only two of them. They couldn't even make a dent in the capsule.

Mojo let out an evil cackle. He pulled a lever inside the capsule, sending out a bright white ray. It smashed both Girls back into the wall. "Ha-ha-ha-ha! At last I will defeat you!" Mojo cried. "At last I will be victorious! At last —"

But suddenly, there was a tremendous crash. A figure came flying into the room and landed on what was left of Mojo's desk. It was Buttercup!

Buttercup crossed her arms. "Evildoers beware —" she began.

"Oh, no!" Blossom groaned.

"Not again!" Bubbles wailed.

Buttercup grinned. "Evildoers beware — *Buttercup Powerpuff* is here!" She shot toward Mojo's capsule, throwing punches at top speed.

Mojo's capsule cracked and fell into pieces. Mojo's evil smile drooped into a frightened frown.

"Yay!" Bubbles cheered.

"Come on, Girls! Let's get him!" Blossom yelled.

Together, the three Powerpuff Girls went after Mojo. They power-punched him and triple-zapped him with their eye beams. They baseball-blasted him and victoryvolleyed him until he could fight no more.

"And now," Buttercup announced, "this is to make sure you never broadcast another  cartoon ever again!" With her superpowered green eye beams, she blasted the twenty TV sets on the wall. Finally, she burned huge holes in the walls of the tower itself. Then she turned to her sisters. "Come on, Girls! We've got a lot of people to save!"

Buttercup, Blossom, and Bubbles spent the rest of the day battling evil. It was tough going, but together, the trio was able to do it. Finally, every monster was defeated, every criminal was behind bars, and every citizen was safe at home.

When they were done, Blossom turned to Buttercup. "It's great to have you back," she said. "What made you snap out of it?"

"It was weird," Buttercup replied. "I was standing there in front of the TV store when suddenly all the screens went blank." She shrugged. "Technical difficulties, I guess."

Blossom exchanged glances with Bubbles. "Yeah, I guess so."

"Anyway, I realized I was getting kind of bored watching someone else fight," Buttercup finished. "I wanted to get back into the action myself."

"Just in time," Blossom said. "Bubbles and I were getting really tired of trying to protect Townsville all by ourselves."

"Yeah," Bubbles agreed. "And we were

getting pretty tired of hearing everyone ask us where you were, too."

"It's great to be back," Buttercup said. "And I promise never to let a cartoon take over my life like that again!"

"Good!" Blossom sighed. "Phew, what a day!"

"I know," Bubbles agreed. "I'm exhausted."

"Let's all go home and relax," Buttercup suggested. "I wonder if there's anything good on TV?"

Oh, Buttercup, not again!

And so, once again, the day was saved, thanks to all THREE of The Powerpuff Girls.